Twilight's
Grand Finale

UNICORN
University

#5

Twilight's
Grand Finale

★ by DAISY SUNSHINE ★
illustrated by MONIQUE DONG

ALADDIN
New York London Toronto Sydney New Delhi

ALADDIN
An imprint of Simon & Schuster Children's Publishing Division
1230 Avenue of the Americas, New York, New York 10020
First Aladdin paperback edition February 2022
Text copyright © 2022 by Simon & Schuster, Inc.
Illustrations copyright © 2022 by Monique Dong
Also available in an Aladdin hardcover edition.
All rights reserved, including the right of reproduction in whole or in part in any form.
ALADDIN and related logo are registered trademarks of Simon & Schuster, Inc.
For information about special discounts for bulk purchases, please contact Simon & Schuster
Special Sales at 1-866-506-1949 or business@simonandschuster.com.
The Simon & Schuster Speakers Bureau can bring authors to your live event. For more information or to
book an event contact the Simon & Schuster Speakers Bureau at 1-866-248-3049 or visit our website
at www.simonspeakers.com.
Book designed by Laura Lyn DiSiena
The illustrations for this book were rendered digitally.
The text of this book was set in Tinos.
Manufactured in the United States of America 0122 OFF
2 4 6 8 10 9 7 5 3 1
Library of Congress Cataloging-in-Publication Data
Names: Sunshine, Daisy, author. | Dong, Monique, illustrator.
Title: Twilight's grand finale / by Daisy Sunshine ; illustrated by Monique Dong.
Description: First Aladdin paperback edition. | New York : Aladdin, 2022. |
Series: Unicorn University | Summary: When her original plan goes up in smoke, Twilight must prove
to herself—and her older sisters—that she can come up with another magical way to end the university's
annual carnival.
Identifiers: LCCN 2021023873 (print) | LCCN 2021023874 (ebook) |
ISBN 9781665900973 (pbk) | ISBN 9781665900980 (hc) | ISBN 9781665900997 (ebook)
Subjects: CYAC: Unicorns—Fiction. | Self-reliance—Fiction. | Boarding schools—Fiction. | Schools—
Fiction. | LCGFT: Novels.
Classification: LCC PZ7.1.S867 Ty 2022 (print) | LCC PZ7.1.S867 (ebook) | DDC [Fic]—dc23
LC record available at https://lccn.loc.gov/2021023873
LC ebook record available at https://lccn.loc.gov/2021023874

For lovers of sparkles, rainbows, and magic

CONTENTS

Rainbow Balloons

Twilight looked down at her painter's smock and snorted in surprise. She was totally covered in paint! Her deep black coat was speckled with a rainbow of colors, and her hooficure was covered by blue and pink splotches. *Actually,* she thought, *this is a cool idea for a painting.* She imagined a big canvas filled with splattered colors.

But Twilight's dreams of future art projects were put on pause when a bright orange unicorn came running up to her. A giant cluster of colorful balloons bobbed behind them, and Twilight noticed the strings were tied to the unicorn's horn.

"Hi, Sunny," Twilight said. "So cool—it looks like you're pulling a rainbow behind you."

Sunny stopped to catch their breath. "Thanks!" they said, still panting from the run over. "Where"—*huff*—"do you"—*huff*—"want them?"

Twilight bit her lip and tried to remember which booth needed balloons. She had been juggling so many tasks that

she was losing track of things! Being in charge of all the decorations for the Unicorn University Annual Carnival meant that Twilight was responsible for everything from balloon decisions to booth painting to fireworks!

Unicorns from all over Sunshine Springs, and even some who lived in other parts of the five kingdoms, were traveling to Unicorn University for the celebration. Parents and siblings of current students would arrive tomorrow to visit with students and see the campus. Every year, the first years planned and set up the events of the carnival, meaning it was Twilight's class's turn. They had spent weeks thinking up game ideas, snacks, and, most exciting of all, a big surprise to end the night. The carnival was a tradition, and Twilight wanted this carnival to be one to remember.

"At the welcome tent!" Twilight finally remembered. That's where the balloons needed to go! "I can bring them over, Sunny. Why don't you take a snack break? The baking club made special apple cakes for everyone."

Sunny smiled wide. "You're the best, Twilight." They bent down their horn so Twilight could take the balloons, and then they jogged off in search of sweets.

When the art club had first asked Twilight to be in charge of decorations, she had thought they'd made a mistake. If someone had told her on her very first day at Unicorn University that she would be telling any other unicorn what to do, she would have whinnied in their face. But when she thought about the carnival, her big imagination took over and she couldn't help but think of all the ways to make things look beautiful. It had been her idea to have different clubs decorate their booths with materials they loved most, and the result was perfect. Twilight looked at the booths around her. The garden club had decorated their booth with flowers; the science club had made a bubble machine that was burping up big, soapy bubbles; and the baking club had hung doughnuts and cookies at their booth.

Over at the baking booth, where Sunny was happily

munching on apple cake, Twilight noticed that Comet, one of her best friends, was using her flying ability to frost the top of a giant cake with her horn. Twilight chuckled. Comet looked so serious, but she was totally covered in frosting! It made for a silly sight.

The balloons above Twilight's head bopped together as the wind whipped up, reminding her to get moving. As she walked toward the blue-and-white-striped welcome tent, the springtime smell of fresh flowers and sunshine wafted through the air, and the green grass under her hooves squished a little from the morning rain. Feeling lighter than air, Twilight skipped the rest of the way.

As she tied the balloons to one of the welcome tent's poles, she heard a very familiar voice. And it did *not* sound very happy.

"One at a time! One at time!" a mint-colored unicorn yelled to a crowd of first years. It was Twilight's other good friend Shamrock, and she could see that his glasses were crooked and his mane was a mess. Twilight knew that the more rumpled Shamrock looked, the more ruffled he felt. *Uh-oh*, Twilight thought, *something must be wrong*. After finishing off her knot, Twilight headed over to help figure out the problem.

2

Maps and Magic

"B ut I thought my booth was going to be here!"

"Didn't we say the dunk tank was in the middle?"

"The dunk tank can't be the middle! That's where the stage is."

The first years around Shamrock were shouting so loudly over each other that Twilight wondered how they could hear themselves think. And from what she'd heard so far, she had a feeling she knew what they were shouting about. Shamrock had a photographic memory, and so everyone was used to asking him where things were supposed to go, but on the day before the carnival, there were simply too many questions for one unicorn to answer. Twilight could see the problem was that he couldn't be everywhere at once to remind everyone what they had planned, which meant groups and clubs were clashing and literally stepping on each other's hooves!

Too bad we can't copy his brain, she thought.

But wait! While they couldn't clone Shamrock, they might be able to do something else. . . .

Twilight used her special ability to turn invisible to get Shamrock's attention. She had learned that unicorns would take notice if she shimmered in and out really fast. It wasn't quite disappearing—it was more like she was glittering.

Shamrock glanced her way, and a look of relief crossed his face. In fact, he looked at Twilight like she was a super-hero. "Any ideas?"

Twilight's eyes sparkled. "Why don't you draw a map,

Shamrock? Then everyone can make a copy, and be on the same page. Literally!"

The whole group laughed. It was so obvious! Shamrock got to work drawing, and the other unicorns pulled out pens and paper to copy his sketch.

"Thanks, Twilight!" one of the unicorns called as they bent over a piece of paper.

"What would we do without you?" another unicorn mumbled, a pencil dangling from the side of her mouth.

Twilight smiled to herself, feeling like she was filled with sunshine. Not only was she decorating the whole fair, but she was solving problems, too! She remembered a famous painting she had seen once of a unicorn smiling. Her mom had said it looked like the unicorn had a secret, but Twilight didn't think that was it. As she stood in the field looking around at all her classmates' hard work, Twilight thought she finally understood what the unicorn in the painting was smiling about. The unicorn was proud of herself!

At first Twilight had been nervous about taking charge of the carnival decorations. She didn't think she was smart like Shamrock, or funny like Comet, and she certainly didn't have big adventures like her other best friend, Sapphire. But over the last few weeks Twilight had learned that she was good at helping other unicorns. And that made her happy.

Twilight noticed how the balloons at the welcome booth bobbed and dipped with the wind, and they now reminded her of the puffball flowers that had sprouted all over Unicorn University. Round, white, and about the size of one of her hooves, puffballs popped up at the start of spring, but they never stayed for more than a week, and soon the wind would blow the balls apart and spread the flowers' seeds all over Sunshine Springs. Twilight loved them, and she was glad they were around for the carnival. Some unicorns said if you made a wish and blew on one, your wish would come true. Twilight looked down to see a puffball right at her hoof. She leaned down, and her breath sent the puffball's seeds floating through the air. *I hope we have the perfect carnival*, she wished.

Straightening up, Twilight saw her friend Sapphire struggling to tie down a purple tent. The wind was getting really strong, and the tent looked like it was about to fly away—and carry Sapphire with it! Twilight rushed over to help.

"Thank you!" Sapphire huffed when Twilight grabbed on to the rope. The two of them pulled and pulled. Finally they were able to tie the rope to a nearby tree and secure the tent.

Catching her breath, Sapphire swung her blue braids out of her face and looked around the grounds. "As Comet would say, everything looks glitter-tastic."

Twilight laughed. "It sure does!" she said as the wind brushed her cheek.

"You know, we couldn't have done any of this without you," Sapphire said.

Twilight smiled like the unicorn in the painting. "Thanks,

Sapphire. I love how everything came together, but I'm most excited for the grand finale tomorrow."

Out of everything at the carnival, Twilight was proudest of the fireworks display they had planned. Some classes performed plays, and others had circus performances with acrobats, but Twilight couldn't think of a better way to end than with beautiful fireworks.

"I can't believe Stella's great-aunt designs fireworks," Sapphire said. "She must be so cool."

Stella and her partner, Celest, were in charge of food for all the unicorns at Unicorn University. Twilight had learned on her very first day—when she'd turned invisible and couldn't turn back!—that they always had good advice and even better food. Twilight, Shamrock, Sapphire, and especially Comet visited Stella and Celest often, and not only when they were looking for snacks. Stella was a dragon and told the most amazing stories. She had grown up in Cloud Kingdom with other dragons but had traveled all over the world. One time Stella had told Twilight and her friends all about her great-aunt Beatrice, one of the greatest fireworks designers in all the five kingdoms. When Twilight had heard the story, it had been like a lightbulb had turned on, and she'd known they would have to bring Ms. Beatrice to Unicorn University for the carnival.

It had taken a lot of convincing, though. First she'd convinced Headmaster Starblaze to allow them to have fire-works, and *then* she'd had to write a very convincing letter to the great fireworks maker herself. Twilight thought fireworks were so magical, not just because they were beautiful but because they seemed to bring unicorns together. Everyone was amazed all at once. What was more magical than that?

"We're really going to end this party with a show," Twilight told Sapphire now.

"With a bang!" Sapphire chuckled. "Hey, when does your family get here?"

"They get here in the morning," Twilight told her. "What about you?"

"My mom and sisters will be here tomorrow afternoon," Sapphire groaned. "Don't get me wrong, I'm excited to see them. But all four little foals running around here? I hope they don't tear down the Crystal Library."

Twilight laughed. "The Crystal Library is older than Sunshine Springs. I think it will survive."

"You clearly don't know my sisters very well," Sapphire said, rolling her eyes. "You're lucky you have older siblings."

Twilight bit her bottom lip. Truthfully, she was worried about seeing Dusk and Sunset. She wanted them to be proud of her and see how grown-up she was now. "I want everything to be perfect. I hope they like the carnival. . . ." Suddenly Twilight was nervous. Her sisters had always been larger than life. Dusk was the smartest unicorn Twilight had ever met, and Sunset had been the captain of the hoofball team at Unicorn University, not to mention the most popular unicorn in her class. Compared to them, Twilight couldn't help but feel small. *What will they think of my decorations?* she worried.

"Of course they'll love it!" Sapphire said. "I bet they'll just be happy to see you."

Twilight nodded, but she couldn't ignore that butterflies had started bouncing around in her tummy. *The carnival is going to be perfect*, she tried to tell herself. It had to be.

3

The Sisters' Song

The next morning Twilight woke up to the sound of familiar voices.

"Where's my little sister?"

"Helloooooo, Twilight! We're heeerrre!"

"Girls, please. You're going to wake the whole stable."

"The whole stable? I think all of Sunshine Springs heard them."

Twilight laughed at her family's loud arrival. Normally it took forever for Twilight to wake up and start the day—she was not usually a morning unicorn. But she was so excited to see everyone that she jumped right up, shook off her blanket, and went galloping out of the stable.

"You're here!" Twilight squealed when she reached her parents and two sisters.

Her family cheered as they huddled around her. Twilight felt as if she were floating on air. It was so good to see them!

After Twilight nuzzled everyone hello, she stepped back and took in the morning. The sun was still rising and the air was crisp and cool, so Twilight stamped her hooves to warm up. She watched the wind blow through the tree limbs around her, the branches shaking as if they were trying to warm themselves up too.

"What time does the carnival start, Twilight?" her dad asked.

"Four thirty," her sister Dusk replied. "Don't worry, Twilight. I read the pamphlet on the way." Dusk was the most serious of the sisters, even though she also told the best jokes. She was also the neatest. Her dark gray coat was never anything but perfectly shiny, and she wore her mane in a row of four tight buns. She said it was more practical that way, since then she didn't have to worry about her hair getting in the way of things.

"Oh," Twilight said, "I'm not worried—"

"I read the pamphlet too, you know," her other sister, Sunset, interrupted. "Did you see that they're having fire-works?" Sunset had a deep purple coat with white spots, almost like the cloudy night sky. Sunset liked to wear her white mane loose and flowing.

"The fireworks are something we—" Twilight tried to say, but she was thwarted again!

"I didn't see the special song scheduled, though, Twilight," Dusk said, her eyebrows arched as if Twilight had made some big mistake.

Twilight felt her cheeks heat up. *Did I miss something?* She was sure she had double-checked with her classmates that the pamphlet had all the activities listed, but she had no idea what the special song was. *Will someone's feelings be hurt if it's left out?* Twilight felt a pit in her stomach open up, and her hooves shimmered in and out of invisibility.

"What special song are you talking about?" Twilight asked, her voice squeaking a little.

"When I was a first year," Dusk started, "a few of us wrote and performed this song about the school, and—"

"Then in *my* first year, we sang the song and created a special dance, too. Unicorns couldn't stop talking about it," Sunset said with a mane flip.

Before Twilight could say anything, the two of them started singing.

"When you're at Unicorn University,
Your troubles will be few and far between!"

Twilight let out a deep breath. Nothing was ruined after all. She shook her head and tried not to get grumpy with her older sisters. She didn't want to ruin the day, but a voice inside her head was wondering why her sisters always had

to be the center of attention. She wished they would listen to her sometimes. *They think they know everything.*

"Come on, Twilight," Dusk said. "We need your soprano."

"Yeah," Sunset added. "We sound silly without you."

Twilight just smiled. She didn't think it was *her* fault they sounded silly.

Catching her look, her sisters started laughing, and Twilight finally joined in with them. The knot in her stomach loosened as they giggled together. It almost felt like they were back home on the family farm.

Then the wind whipped again, and the trees started shaking their leaves all around her. Twilight looked to where the carnival was set up on the Looping Lawn, suddenly worried the strong winds would knock something over. But everything looked as they'd left it the day before.

In the distance Twilight could see two dragons standing on the big hill that overlooked the carnival. Even from far away Twilight knew the green dragon was Stella, and she guessed the gray dragon with her was Stella's great-aunt, the master fireworks designer!

"Oh—" Twilight squeaked, nerves getting the best of her. "I want to go check in with Stella. I'll be right—"

"Oh, fantastic! I'll come too," Sunset said, throwing back her mane like a movie star. "That's the school chef you talk about in your letters home, right?"

"Ooh, I wonder if she'd be interested in hearing about my apple trees," Dusk said. Dusk was a scientist working on a special apple tree that could grow in any of the five kingdoms. Although, apple trees grew all over Unicorn University, and Twilight couldn't see why Stella would need any more, but she couldn't think of a nice way to say that. Twilight scraped her hoof against the grass and tried to take a deep, calming breath. *They're doing it again! Making everything about them!*

It was Twilight who had been coordinating the fireworks with Stella for weeks. She worried it would look like she wasn't confident if her big sisters tagged along—like she didn't know what she was doing. But Twilight couldn't tell her sisters she wanted to go alone, could she? She didn't want to hurt their feelings.

"Mom? Dad? Did you want to meet Stella too?" Sunset asked. Twilight grimaced. Now her parents were coming?

"You know, I think I see some old friends coming our way," her mother said, waving at two unicorns with long, wavy gray manes who were walking toward the stables.

"We can catch up with you fillies later," Twilight's dad added.

"Dew! Beam!" Twilight's mother called out, and soon the adults were chatting away about the party.

"Just us, then," Dusk said, leading the charge up the hill. Twilight sighed and took her place behind her sisters as they made their way to the dragons.

4

Meeting Ms. Beatrice

"Twilight!" Stella called, raising a sparkling, green scale-covered arm above her head. Twilight noticed she had left her apron in the kitchen and was free of flour dust for once. And her claws were painted purple! Twilight wasn't sure she'd ever seen Stella so put together.

The other dragon's gray scales did not sparkle like Stella's. She peered over her small wire-rimmed glasses, staring at them as if she were trying to see right through them. Twilight noticed that her sisters held their horns higher under her gaze. Twilight stood a little straighter too.

"This is my aunt, Ms. Beatrice," Stella told them.

"Thank you so much for coming, Ms. Beatrice," Twilight said, her voice coming out barely louder than a whisper. "We're all excited about your fireworks." Standing between Ms. Beatrice and her two sisters made Twilight feel like she had shrunk to the size of a fairy.

Ms. Beatrice wrinkled her nose and snorted smoke rings from her nostrils. Twilight watched the rings grow and grow before they were taken by the wind and floated down through the valley. *That can't be good*, Twilight thought.

Stella jumped in to explain. "Aunt Beatrice has been measuring the wind and, well . . . Oh, I'm so sorry, Twilight."

"*Never* apologize for the wind," Ms. Beatrice said, drawing her long black claws to her chest as if Stella had said the worst thing in the five kingdoms.

Stella hung her head and looked at her feet. "Sorry,

Auntie." Twilight couldn't believe this was the same loud, funny, confident Stella she had come to know on her very first day at Unicorn University. This Stella was a totally different dragon!

Ms. Beatrice snorted again, but only a wisp of smoke came out this time. "We must respect the skies. No fireworks today," she said simply.

Twilight felt wobbly on her hooves. No fireworks? But that was supposed to be the best part of the party! Twilight was stunned. She didn't know what to say.

Dusk, ever the serious scientist, bobbed her horn in a nod. "I see. Those fireworks would be less show and more like . . ." Her sister looked around for the right word. "Fireballs?"

Well, so much for "serious scientist." But Dusk's word choice did paint a clear picture.

Twilight imagined a fireball hurtling at the crowd, and groaned.

Sunset laughed and looked at her younger sister. "Cheer up, Twilight! There's still the rest of the carnival."

Twilight nodded, though she couldn't ignore the giant lump in her throat. She tried to push the disappointment away, but she felt like she was letting her classmates down. Even if it wasn't her fault and was because of the wind.

The whole carnival was like a play, with lots of different people playing different parts, and it all came together into something beautiful. Now it was as if Twilight didn't have the right costume or had knocked down the set.

Dusk nudged her. "Don't worry, Twilight."

"*Always* worry about the wind," Ms. Beatrice said with a serious look at Twilight. "Now, Stella, show me your rooms."

"Follow me, Auntie." Stella led her aunt down the hill, but she looked back at Twilight, saying a silent "Sorry" over her shoulder. Twilight smiled and shrugged in response.

"Really, Twilight," Sunset said. "It's no big deal. It's only fireworks. Don't make a huge thing out of this."

Sunset was trying to help, but it made Twilight feel like she was being silly for being sad. That made Twilight feel even worse.

"Really, you're too sensitive," Dusk said. "I'm sorry to say it, but disappointment is a part of life."

Twilight could feel tears welling up. She shook her head, trying to stop them from spilling over. *Am I just being a little foal?* she worried. *And all I wanted was for my sisters to see how much I've changed.*

Twilight pushed past her sisters, not wanting them to see the waterfall that was surely going to flood down her cheeks any minute now. She headed down the hill. "There's a carnival meeting. I have to go," she mumbled.

Her sisters did not take the hint. Instead they galloped after her, and soon flanked her. Twilight saw that each of them wore a big, fake smile.

"All you need is a better attitude, Little Sister," Dusk said.

"I agree, the best offense is a good defense!" Sunset told her.

"For every action there is an equal and opposite reaction," Dusk added, nodding.

Twilight had no idea what they were talking about.

"You need to come up with a new plan!" Sunset told her.

"When you present to the group, all you have to say is that there won't be any fireworks, but there'll be something else," Dusk said.

Twilight mumbled, "We usually vote on new decisions, and I don't—"

"We know how much you worry about things," Dusk interrupted.

"And how much you hate talking to groups," Sunset added. "So we've got this. You're a sensitive unicorn, we know how easily you get upset. But don't worry. We're here."

"By the time we get to the meeting," Dusk said, "we'll have a new plan of action."

Twilight looked down and noticed that her hooves had completely disappeared. *Oh no*, she worried. She hadn't lost control of her power of invisibility like this since the first day of school. *Am I growing backward?*

5

Dancing Puffballs

The wind was strong as the three sisters walked toward the carnival grounds. Twilight stayed quiet and listened to the grass rustle and the trees whisper. She noticed that the puffball flowers didn't make any sounds at all. They just danced to nature's music. But they were still part of things. They still stood out.

The three fillies were early to the carnival grounds, and things were quiet and calm. "Give me a minute, okay?" Twilight asked her sisters softly. For once they listened.

Her sisters let her wander off alone, and Twilight took

a few calming breaths. She closed her eyes and focused on the sun on her face. Feeling better after a few moments, she opened her eyes to see her hooves reappear on the bright green grass, and she smiled. *Okay, one crisis over.*

Twilight walked around the booths to check on the decorations before everyone else arrived. She didn't want there to be any more surprises and was happy to find that everything was in order. The painted signs were dry, the daisy chains were hung, and the balloons were brightly colored and flying high.

Soon the other first years made their way to the carnival's stage, which was at the center of everything. Twilight saw they were all laughing and smiling. They wouldn't be so happy and excited after they heard the news about the wind and no fireworks. Twilight felt like a big raincloud right before it sent everyone inside with a storm.

When everyone had arrived, Twilight made her way up to the stage and called for attention with her special shimmer. But when she said "Hi, everyone," her voice was too quiet to get everyone focused. She cleared her throat for another attempt, but her sisters jumped in to help before she could try again.

"QUIET!" Sunset screamed to the crowd.

"Circle round. Twilight's speaking," Dusk added in her sternest voice.

Twilight felt her cheeks flare up. She tried to give them a look to say, *Please stop talking*, but they only gave her big smiles, as if they had been some huge help.

"We're Twilight's sisters," Sunset continued, looking all the first years over.

"So listen up," Dusk added with a tap of her hoof.

Twilight held back a groan. Now was not the time for this! She took a few steps away from her sisters and looked over to the other first years. "I just found out that it's too windy for fireworks and we have to respect the wind or else there will be um . . . fireballs." That was all she could get out before all the first years started talking at once. Everyone seemed upset, confused, and disappointed.

Twilight took a deep breath, trying to gather her thoughts. And her courage. "So, we have to figure out—"

"But don't you worry!" Sunset cut in with a smile, stepping toward Twilight.

"Because we have a plan," Dusk added, coming to the other side of Twilight.

"We'll teach you guys our song and dance!" they said in unison.

Twilight could feel her cheeks get so warm that it felt like they were on fire. Then she looked down at her hooves to see they were completely invisible again! If she hadn't been squished between her sisters, she would have run away.

"Now, who would like to sing?" Dusk asked the crowd, using her best teacher voice.

"And who loves to dance?" Sunset said, doing some sort of weaving side step.

Not seeing how she could wrench the spotlight back from her sisters, Twilight used this opportunity to escape. Luckily, Sunset and Dusk were too busy taking over—gathering singers and dancers—to notice her slip away. Twilight didn't think anyone would even realize she was gone.

She wondered how everything had gone so . . .

imperfectly. The fireworks were supposed to have been her masterpiece! She had been so proud of herself for thinking of the plan, and she had worked really hard with Stella to make sure it would all come together. No other class had done something so big before. And now that fireworks weren't a safe option, she wished she were allowed to try to fix it without her sisters butting in.

My sisters think I'm useless, Twilight thought. *They think I can't do anything without their help.*

Twilight sighed. Maybe Sunset and Dusk were right.

Wanting to be alone, Twilight slipped into full invisibility and decided to go for a walk. Without knowing quite where her hooves were taking her, she walked and walked until she found herself nearly at Stella and Celest's kitchen, and she smiled when she saw the cottage attached to the big oak tree. The crooked chimney always made her think of a top hat, as if the house were all dressed up. Twilight willed herself visible and hurried across the lawn.

She knew she would find a cup of tea and a sugary treat inside. *Exactly what I need.*

But when she pushed open the red door, she was surprised to see not just a pot of tea and a pile of cookies but Comet, Sapphire, and Shamrock all waiting around the big wooden table.

Twilight felt like she could cry from happiness, but instead she asked, "What are you guys doing here? Where's Stella and Celest?"

"Well, Stella and Celest had to bring Old Ms. Cranky on a tour of Unicorn University," Comet said, rolling her eyes.

"Comet!" Shamrock said, his mouth dropping open. "You can't say that! Ms. Beatrice is *the* best fireworks designer in the five kingdoms. She deserves our respect."

Sapphire shrugged. "I don't know, she *did* seem pretty cranky to me."

Twilight laughed so hard that she could feel the knot in her stomach start to come undone. She shook her head and beamed at her friends. "I'm so happy to see you all."

"We had a feeling you'd end up here," Sapphire said.

"So we asked Stella and Celest if we could wait inside," Comet explained.

"There's chocolate chip cookies," Shamrock told her, pointing to the center of the table. "Your favorite!"

Twilight settled in at the table and bit into a cookie. "This day has turned out to be the worst." She shook her head and looked at her friends. She felt better knowing they would listen and try to help. That's what they did for each other. It was a comfort just to know they were there for her. "My sisters don't think I can do anything on my own." She took another bite of the cookie. "And I'm worried that they're right," she said with her mouth full and tears in her eyes.

Her friends huddled around her.

"That's *so* not true. Twilight, you've made this the best. Carnival. Ever," Comet said.

"The booths would never have looked as cool as they do without your ideas," Shamrock said.

"I think your sisters mean well," Sapphire said gently. "They're probably trying to help. I can be like that when my little sisters need help."

"You think I need help too?" Twilight said. Now she was full-on wailing.

"No, no," Comet piped up. "Just a new plan, I guess?"

Twilight hung her horn. *Maybe I should give up and let my sisters do the whole dance thing. Then I could stop worrying.*

"I don't think dancing and singing will be as cool as fireworks," Shamrock said seriously. "But I do think we need something to end the carnival. It's tradition."

"We need to go out with a bang," Sapphire said.

Comet looked thoughtful. "It's probably too late to bake the kingdom's largest cake, but . . ."

"What I liked about the fireworks was that it was something we could all watch together," Twilight said. "They're magical."

"If only we could make fireworks that didn't turn into fireballs!" Comet said.

Sapphire chuckled. "Like a show in the sky, but not made of fire."

Twilight looked up quickly. That was it! "You mean like balloons?" Her heart was beating fast, and she started to feel jumpy on her hooves. She might just have the perfect plan. But could she pull it off? She felt her tears dry on her cheeks as she looked up with a sniffle.

"I don't think we have enough balloons," Shamrock said. "And the environmental impact . . ."

"Oh, of course," Twilight said, nodding. "But what about something *like* balloons? Like . . . puffball flowers?"

Twilight watched as her friends' faces went from confused to excited. They got it!

"They're everywhere right now! The grounds are full of them," Comet shouted. Well, it was really a normal volume for Comet—her voice tended to be a bit louder than most.

"And if we dust them with bright colored powder and throw them from the hill above the carnival, they should float in the wind just like a fireworks display," Shamrock said. He scrunched his big, bushy eyebrows as he did the calculations in his head.

"We have to tell everyone!" Sapphire said. "Should we go club by club?"

Twilight nodded. "That sounds good. I'll tell my sisters and the dancers. But . . ." Twilight paused, pushing around some cookie crumbs left on the table, to avoid looking at her friends. "Do you think my sisters will be mad at me?"

Comet waved her hoof as if to wave Twilight's worry away. "They should've asked for your opinion in the first place!"

Maybe she's right, Twilight thought, but she still couldn't shake the feeling that she was doing something wrong. Would Dusk and Sunset understand?

6

Breaking the News

Comet waved from the cottage as Twilight, Sapphire, and Shamrock left on their missions. The baking club was meeting at the kitchen soon, so she would be able to fill the members in on the new plan. Meanwhile, Shamrock would head off to the greenhouses to meet with the garden club, and Sapphire would go to the Friendly Fields so she could talk to her hoofball teammates. The plan was to ask their classmates to collect bunches of puffball flowers when they went back to the carnival, and spread the word to all the other first years. Luckily, there were puffballs everywhere!

Twilight made her way to the Looping Lawn, feeling nervous because her job was to break the news of the puff-ball plan to her sisters. Twilight's hooves were shimmering in and out of invisibility, and her stomach felt like there was a storm inside. Growing up, her sisters had seemed like two lions, and she had felt like a quiet mouse. It hadn't bothered her so much before, because being a mouse had felt like her role in the family. After everything she had learned at Unicorn University, she didn't want to be a mouse any longer. But being around her sisters made her feel like she was stuck being small and squeaky, and she didn't know how she was going to stand up to her two roaring sisters. Twilight dreaded what they would say.

She dragged her heavy hooves up the hill toward her sisters and the group of unicorns learning a simple dance on the stage. Twilight stopped to listen to the song and found herself swaying to the tune. It reminded her of something they would sing at home. The dance was pretty easy too, with simple hoof waving and horn swaying. Twilight's sisters spotted her and waved her over to the group.

"What do you think?" Dusk asked.

"Don't you just love it?" Sunset squealed.

"It is actually pretty cool," Twilight told them, and she did think it was a fun song and dance. She could imagine the whole crowd joining in, since it was pretty easy to learn. It was fun to see what her sisters had done when they were at school, but Twilight still wanted her grand finale to be unique. Something special.

Dusk laughed. "You sound surprised."

"Kind of," Twilight admitted. She hoofed the ground, bringing up the dirt below the bright green grass. It took a lot for Twilight to not simply run away and leave a note.

"I have some news," Twilight made herself say. She took a deep breath, and for once her sisters didn't interrupt. "We have a new plan. Something else to replace the fireworks. Other than a dance."

Sunset tilted her head with surprise. "What do you mean?"

"Puffballs!" Twilight squeaked, and then cleared her throat. "Sorry, I mean, all the first years are going to collect puffball flowers, we'll color them, and then we'll all release them at the same time from the higher hill, the one where we met with Stella this morning. Then the wind will carry them

through the valley almost like flower fireworks!" Twilight was smiling now, all the words rushing out at once. *They have to see how great this idea is!*

"So, what about this song we've been working on *all* afternoon?" Dusk asked. She was frowning, her eyebrows drawn together in a way that made Twilight shuffle her hooves nervously.

"And the dance?" Sunset said. "Your classmates have been working hard on this, too!"

Twilight looked over to the group of unicorns, feeling guilty. She hadn't thought about that.

One of her classmates, Peppermint, tossed her red-and-white mane with her signature mane flip and said, "We can still do the dance and song, right? We can do both. I mean . . . duh?"

Twilight smiled, relieved. "Yes! Good idea, Peppermint. The dance can be performed earlier."

"Hmph! You mean while everyone is playing games at

the carnival?" Dusk asked. Twilight noticed that her buns had become slightly undone. *Uh-oh*.

"And eating cakes? This dance is meant to be *seen*!" Sunset said.

"Really, Twilight," Dusk said angrily. "We've been doing this for you. We saw how upset you were, and we helped because we're your sisters."

"Now suddenly the plan has changed?" Sunset whined. "I mean, I had other plans for the day. You know, growing up means respecting other people's time, Twilight."

Twilight felt her face flush. This was not about them! Couldn't they see that Twilight's plan was better? Couldn't they just be happy for her? Why did they shove the fact that she was younger into her face? "You can't force everyone to do what you want. Not everyone is your little sister," Twilight said, and stomped her hooves. She had to admit, stomping her hooves did feel childish, but she was so angry! *How can they not understand?*

"Excuse me?" Sunset asked. "I can't believe how selfish you're being."

"Really, this is not the Twilight we know," Dusk added.

"Guess we should just go. Come on, Dusk," Sunset said, giving Twilight a look as cold as Ms. Beatrice's.

Twilight watched her sisters walk away, not knowing what to say. That had not gone as planned.

She felt terrible.

7

Splashing Rocks

S ooo . . . ," Peppermint said. "Want to fill us in on this puffball plan?"

"Ask Sapphire," Twilight told her as she stomped away from the lawn. *She's better at this anyway.*

A totally invisible Twilight broke into a gallop. The wind whipped her mane around her face as big, hot tears fell from her eyes. *This day isn't even close to perfect! It is the opposite of perfect!*

She stomped over to the stream where a willow tree the size of a stable grew on the bank. Still angry, Twilight kicked a few pebbles into the water. It felt good to watch them splash and plop into the stream. She went to look for some bigger rocks but was interrupted by a familiar voice.

"Is that Twilight, or an angry ghost?" a sparkling green dragon asked from beneath the willow tree.

"Stella?" Twilight asked, embarrassed that someone had seen her outburst. She had been letting herself act like a filly, but only because she'd thought no one was around. She dropped her invisibility and walked toward Stella.

Stella chuckled as she rumbled her green scaly body over to Twilight. "Aunt Beatrice is taking a nap at the cottage. And I needed some alone time," she explained.

Twilight nodded. "I get that."

"How's it going with your sisters?" Stella asked.

"It's terrible," Twilight said with fresh tears. Stella's question had unleashed a new flood of emotion. "They think I'm a little filly who doesn't know anything," Twilight blubbered. "And maybe they're right."

"You know how much you're capable of, Twilight," Stella said. "You have created this wonderful carnival. The fireworks were only the candles on the cake. The cake itself will still be . . . delicious. Hmm, got a bit lost in my metaphor there, but you know what I mean."

Twilight giggled through her tears. "We actually have a new plan to replace the fireworks."

"The song and dance?" Stella asked.

"No, puffballs!" Twilight went on to explain the new plan.

"Twilight! That's wonderful! It is better than fireworks. And I'm a dragon," she said. "So I know what I'm talking about."

Twilight smiled before she remembered her sisters. "Dusk and Sunset are really mad, though. They worked hard on the dance and think I don't appreciate them. But I wish they had asked me before taking over."

Stella nodded. "I think maybe you should tell your sisters how you feel."

Twilight played with some rocks at her hooves, before admitting what was bothering her. "I've changed a lot at Unicorn University, you know. What if they don't like this new me? What if they don't want to talk to me anymore?"

"They're your sisters and they love you," Stella said. "No matter what. They will always want to talk to you. And they want you to be yourself."

Twilight had been in enough fights with her sisters to know that wasn't true all the time—Dusk hadn't spoken to Twilight for a week once, after Twilight had accidentally ruined her summer science project—but she understood what Stella was trying to say.

"You know," Stella said, "I haven't had the easiest day myself."

"I'm sorry. Your aunt *is* kind of scary," Twilight said softly.

"You have no idea!" Stella laughed. "She's a big deal in my family. Everyone always does what she says." She shook her head. "All day I've been trying to be someone I'm not."

"She is family, and she loves you. She'll want you to be yourself," Twilight told her with a small smile.

The two of them started laughing. Soon Twilight realized that she didn't want to throw rocks anymore. She wanted to talk to her sisters.

"I'm going to go find Dusk and Sunset," Twilight said.

"And I'm going to find Aunt Beatrice," Stella said. "Think she'd let me call her 'Aunt B'?"

Twilight shook her head. "I wouldn't push it."

"Thank you, Twilight," Stella said, suddenly serious. "For being open with me about your feelings. It helped me figure out my own."

Twilight beamed. Stella was an adult, and Twilight had never thought about an adult needing help before. "Thank you, Stella. I think I know what I need to do now."

The dragon and unicorn hugged before setting out on their journeys.

Twilight searched and searched but couldn't find her

sisters anywhere. She started to worry that they were hiding from her. *They always were better at hide-and-seek*, she thought.

Realizing the time, Twilight made her way back to the carnival. Everything would be starting soon! She had to talk to her classmates. There was one last change she wanted to discuss with them.

"Twilight! Up here!" Shamrock called to her from the hill above the Looping Lawn. Twilight could tell he was surrounded by baskets of colorful puffballs.

"Everything's ready to go! Best carnival ever!" Comet cheered as Twilight got to the top of the hill.

Twilight bit her lower lip. "Almost. I just have one more thing to add."

"Well, I told everyone to meet us here before the carnival. Is everything okay?" Sapphire asked.

"We heard about the big fight with your sisters," Shamrock added.

Twilight groaned. "Is everyone talking about it?"

"Only the first years," Comet said. "But everyone agrees that your sisters were being totally mean."

Twilight shook her head. "I was pretty mean too. But that's what I wanted to talk to you about. I think I have a plan that will make everyone happy."

Twilight looked down at the carnival. She could see the baking club putting out their pies and cookies, the garden club hanging more daisy chains around the stage, the drama club practicing the skit to kick off the carnival. The whole lawn was alive with activity. She could even see guests starting to walk over. It reminded Twilight of a certain kind of painting, the ones that looked all smooshed together and messy when you were up close, but when you stepped back, you could see the whole picture. Up here was a fresh perspective.

8

Showtime!

After what felt like the longest day of Twilight's life, the carnival was finally in full swing. The school band was playing bouncing tunes, and unicorns were laughing all around her. Twilight saw Ms. Beatrice high-five Stella after winning a game at a booth. The two of them were laughing together, and Stella looked like her old self. Twilight was happy to see that Stella's talk with her aunt had gone so well.

Twilight spotted her parents, still chatting away with old friends. She shook her head. She was happy that at least some of her family members were having a good day. She looked around, trying to find her sisters, but couldn't see them anywhere. *Probably avoiding me*, she thought. *I hope this plan works.*

Twilight looked up to see the sun starting to dip in the sky. She'd better get everything moving! She used her special shimmer to make the signal, and the first years closed down their booths and trotted up the hill above the lawn. Well, everyone but Twilight.

Then Headmaster Starblaze climbed the wooden stage at the center of the carnival. He was the biggest unicorn Twilight knew, and his giant hooves shook the stage as he walked over to the microphone. He had to bend his large, shaggy head down way low to reach it.

"Welcome. Welcome home, everyone!" Headmaster Starblaze began. "It is so good to see old friends return to Unicorn University, my favorite place in the five kingdoms. Now let's put our horns together for the first years! This might be the best carnival ever."

Twilight had a feeling he said that every year, but she was still happy as she listened to the crowd tap horns with one another, filling the whole field with twinkling taps. It reminded her of chimes on a windy day.

"And now I'd like to introduce Twilight, who has asked to talk to you all."

It was time. The butterflies in her stomach were putting on a show of their own, flipping and flopping all over the place! Twilight took a deep breath and reminded herself why she was doing this. *For my sisters!*

"Um—hello," she said into the microphone. "We—um—won't be having fireworks tonight. It's too windy."

The crowd grumbled, and Twilight gulped. Would the puffballs be enough?

Twilight felt her courage disappearing as she looked out at the disappointed crowd. Had everyone suddenly grown much bigger than before? Then she saw her sisters waving their horns, off to the side of the crowd. They smiled at her and nodded, supporting her despite everything that had happened. That gave her the confidence she needed. *Maybe I do still need their help sometimes.*

"We have an extra-special surprise planned instead," she said. "But first I'd like to ask my sisters, Dusk and Sunset, to join me onstage."

Sunset and Dusk blinked in surprise, until their friends pushed them toward the stage. Twilight's parents whooped and hollered from their own place in the crowd.

"Please join my sisters and me in a special song about Unicorn University. All you have to do is repeat after us!"

Together the sisters sang the first line, and Twilight could almost imagine they were home at the farm.

> *"When you're at Unicorn University,*
> *Your troubles will be few and far between!*
> *Sunshine and apple trees,*
> *Life is a breeeeeeeze,*
> *When you have friends like these!"*

As the crowd picked up the tune—and some were even following Sunset's dance—Twilight's classmates released the puffballs, and the whole crowd looked up at them floating in the wind. The scene was more beautiful than any fireworks display Twilight could image. The flowers floated down in the wind, their long fuzzy seeds busting apart and flying overhead. It was as if a million tiny umbrellas were floating over the valley.

Just like magic.

9

A Magical Moment

A beautiful sunset filled the sky with soft pinks and purples as the last puffball floated down from the hill. The crowd was silent as they watched it whoosh away with the wind.

Then the first years came laughing and running back to the carnival, and the spell was broken. The once-quiet lawn erupted with unicorns laughing and talking. Twilight herself was caught up in the commotion and was pulled away from her sisters by the other first years, all of them celebrating their successful carnival.

"We did it!" Sapphire cheered.

"Best carnival I've ever been to!" Comet sang as she twirled in circles, her hooves floating off the ground.

"The only carnival you've ever been to," Shamrock pointed out, but Comet only rolled her eyes and kept bouncing around.

"What did it look like from up there?" Twilight asked.

Sapphire scrunched her eyebrows, thinking carefully. "It was like . . ."

"Fireworks?" Shamrock asked with a smile.

Sapphire shook her head. "No . . ."

"Powdered sugar?" Comet asked, recalling their very first day at Unicorn University, when they'd dumped a whole bag of powdered sugar on Twilight.

Sapphire laughed. "No . . ."

"Like magic?" Twilight said. "That's what it looked like from down here."

"Exactly!" Sapphire agreed. "It reminded me of magical fairy dust. Or a rainbow."

"So, what happened with your sisters?" Shamrock asked.

"Well, they sang with me!" Twilight said. "But I haven't had a chance to talk to them yet."

"They'll forgive you," Comet told her. "It's impossible to be mad at you. You're too glitter-tastic."

"She also didn't do anything wrong," Sapphire pointed out.

"That's very true—" Comet stopped short, distracted by something in the distance. "Are those your sisters, Sapphire?" she asked.

All four friends looked over to see four small unicorns climbing on top of the baking booth, trying to get some of the doughnut decorations.

"Oh no!" Sapphire said. "They're going to fall! I have to rescue them!"

Twilight smiled. "Just like a big sister."

"I'll come with you," Comet said. "I have more dough-nuts in a much safer place. Not that I don't understand want-ing to explore new heights." She laughed at her own joke as she galloped after a worried Sapphire.

"I should go find my dads," Shamrock said. "The sun has almost completely set!"

He was right, the sun was so low that the sky had turned a deep purple and the stars were appearing. Unicorn students started to make their way back to the stables, and unicorn visi-tors made their way to their tents, which had been set up around campus. But Twilight couldn't find her sisters or her parents anywhere. She started to worry they had left early without saying goodbye. Could Dusk and Twilight still be mad even though they performed the song *and* released the puffballs?

She hurried back to her stable, her heart feeling like it

was lodged in her throat. *Maybe they left a note*, she hoped.

Then she saw her family all crowded into her stall, and she felt warm from the inside out. Her family didn't see her yet, so for a moment she watched them from afar. The warm glow of the stables lit up their happy faces, and it looked as if they were in an old painting. Out of all the beautiful things Twilight had seen that day, this was the image she wanted to paint most.

"Look at this cute photo!" Sunset squealed, picking up the photo that hung on Twilight's stall from her very first day at Unicorn University. The picture was of her,

Shamrock, Sapphire, and Comet, all smiling and covered in powdered sugar.

"I met her friends earlier today," Dusk said. "A nice herd."

Sunset laughed. "You sound older than Mom and Dad!"

Twilight smiled. Everything seemed so normal. Everyone seemed so happy. Not wanting to be a spectator any longer, she ran down the worn wooden planks as her family's laughter rang through the stable.

"I'm so glad you didn't leave before saying goodbye," she told them, breathless and with tears in her eyes.

"Never!" Sunset said, and Dusk shook her head with a small smile.

"We'll meet you girls outside," their father told them.

"It was a wonderful carnival, Twilight," her mom told her with a nuzzle.

The three sisters were unusually quiet as their parents walked away. Each of them looked at their hooves and around the stables, not quite knowing where to start.

Twilight decided it was up to her. "I'm sorry about today. I should've been honest with you about how I was feeling."

"No—" Sunset started, but Twilight interrupted.

"Wait, that's not all," she continued. "I'm not so little anymore. I don't need you guys to protect me all the time. I just want you to see that I'm grown-up too. Or, well, more grown-up than before." Speeches like this took a lot out of Twilight. She steadied herself with a few deep breaths.

"Twilight, we do see how much you've grown up," Sunset said. Her long white mane waved gently as a breeze swept through the open window. "I think it's hard for us not to jump in when we see you're in trouble. You're our little sister." She nudged Twilight gently with her flank.

"We're sorry we didn't let you figure your problems out by yourself. You should know you can tell us anything. We only want to help," Dusk said.

Twilight smiled up at her sisters, happy tears shining on her cheeks. "You know, I was so nervous about speaking in front of everyone at the carnival," Twilight told them. "I couldn't have done it if you guys hadn't been in the crowd smiling at me."

"She still needs us!" Sunset cheered.

Dusk laughed. "We're really proud of you, Twilight."

"I love you guys," Twilight told them. "And I'll always need you."

Her sisters smiled with tears glittering in their eyes, and the three of them huddled together, nuzzling their noses.

10

Goodbye Tears

The next morning Twilight was once again woken up by the sound of familiar voices.

"Where's my little sister?"

"Helloooooo, Twilight! We're heeerrre!"

"Girls, really."

I guess some things will never change. Twilight rubbed the sleep from her eyes and joined her family outside.

"I will not forget that carnival," her dad told her when she joined them.

"One of the best!" her mom added.

"It was THE best," Dusk said.

"Better than any I've ever been to," Sunset added with a smile.

Twilight looked up at them with a happy grin. "It was magical."

"Sister horn tap?" Dusk asked.

The three sisters did the special secret horn tap they had made up when they were younger.

"When are you going to teach your mom and me that?" Twilight's dad asked. His voice sounded a tad whiney.

"Never!" they all shouted back. That was something they would always agree on. The super-secret horn tap would forever be their special thing.

Twilight said her goodbyes to her family, as they had a long walk ahead of them back to the farm. Feeling happier than ever, she watched them make their way down the dirt path. The carnival might not have been exactly what she'd expected, but it had been perfectly imperfect in the best way.

READ ON FOR A PEEK AT

Sapphire's
Summer Disguise

Dear Sapphire,

We miss you already! Hope you're having the
best time ever. Here are a few things we
think will make you smile. Can't wait to hear
all about your camp adventures!!!

Love,

Comet, Twilight, and Shamrock

S apphire tossed her long blue braids over her shoulder
as she read the note from her very best friends. On the
table in front of her was a big package wrapped in crinkled
brown paper, waiting to be opened.

But she stopped just before tearing off the paper, her hoof

hanging in midair. It felt like someone—or something!—was watching her. The "ghost" she and her friends had met at Sapphire's seaside sleepover had turned out to be a friendly narwhal named Ned, but could the cabin at her summer camp be haunted for real?

Sapphire heard a creak and a whisper, and she looked around the small cabin to see if anyone was there. But all she could see were the wide wooden floorboards and walls made of big tree logs. There were signs that her cabinmates had already arrived, like the towel hanging from one of the hooks, and the stack of magazines on the table, but she was the only unicorn in the cabin. Smiling at herself, Sapphire shrugged her shoulders and brushed it off. *It's probably the wind whistling through the trees*, she thought. *Maybe I'm not used to being in the woods!*

Sapphire had just arrived at Camp Explore in the Great Green Forest of Sunshine Springs, which was far from her home by the ocean. Sapphire was used to the sounds of crashing waves and the salty air of the beach. Here the sounds of birds chirping and the smells of pine trees filled the air. It felt like she was in a different world.

Sapphire had wanted to go to Camp Explore because her hero, Amelia Hoofheart, had gone here when she'd been just a filly. Amelia Hoofheart was a famous unicorn explorer known for her brave adventures. Sapphire wanted to be a famous explorer just like her. *I might be standing just where Amelia Hoofheart once stood!* Sapphire thought. She couldn't help but do a little happy dance on her hooves.

Amelia Hoofheart had flown a hot-air balloon all over the five kingdoms. She had disappeared on her flight to visit the Artic Foxes, and no one had seen her, or her hot-air balloon, for more than twenty years. Sapphire always hoped the explorer would turn up with a grand story to tell. And sometimes Sapphire dreamed of being the unicorn to find Amelia Hoofheart. Then she would be a famous explorer and a hero too.

A well-loved copy of Amelia Hoofheart's autobiography peeked out from Sapphire's overstuffed bag. The cover was peeling at the corners, and the pages were crinkly and brown. But Sapphire still thought the book was perfect.

She carefully pulled it out and flipped to the first chapter. She read the first lines for the one millionth time.

> *Camp Explore was the site of my first adventure. My cabinmates and I were kindred spirits and fast friends. Every day we would try something new. We broke swimming records and ran in the relay races. Every day was a new adventure. We loved planning and playing pranks on each other, other campers, and sometimes even the counselors.*
>
> *One day one of us—we can never remember who—decided to hike to the top of Mount Cliff, so named for its high*

peaks and rocky terrain. It was said that

no camper had made it to the top. We

decided to plant our camp flag on the top

so everyone would know that Camp Explore

had been there first.

We woke up before sunrise, when the

rest of the camp was still slumbering. We

trekked up the mountainside, helping each

other along the way. When we arrived,

sweaty and happy, we cheered as we pulled

out our flag to plant. But all of a sudden

there was a noise from behind us, a small

musical voice saying, "Now, just what do

you think you're doing?"

Sapphire knew the story by heart. A fairy had come to explain that lots of creatures traveled through the mountains, and many more called the top of the mountain their home. There wasn't a flag planted because the mountaintop belonged to everyone. Amelia Hoofheart said that this was when she'd first learned what it meant to be an explorer.

Sapphire loved the story for two reasons.

One, it reminded her of when she'd met Fairy Green. It was at school, at Unicorn University, and she'd helped find the fairy's lost magical dust. That day Sapphire had discovered her magical ability. It wasn't like her friends' magic—she couldn't fly or turn invisible—but Fairy Green had told her that magic came in many forms, and Sapphire's magic was her curiosity and good heart.

And two, Sapphire had always loved the phrase "kindred spirits" that Amelia Hoofheart used. Sapphire had never heard the phrase before reading this book, but she figured it meant "unicorns who felt like friends even if you had never met them before." Her friends back at Unicorn University were kindred spirits, and the four of them had been friends since their very first day at school. And now Sapphire couldn't wait to meet her cabinmates on her very first day of camp!

Sapphire smiled as she turned back to the package her friends had sent. First she pulled out a big white box tied with a yellow ribbon. The sticker on the box said "Curley's Confections." Sapphire knew this must be from Comet, who was spending the summer studying baking with her uncle Curley at his famous bakery right in Celestial City, the capital of Sunshine Springs. He baked cookies for the king and queen! Sapphire opened the box to find a pile of beautiful sugar cookies that *almost* looked too good to eat. They looked like little yellow stars, with sugar crystals blinking in the sunlight.

Munching on a cookie, next Sapphire pulled out a painting of the Crystal Library, her favorite place at Unicorn University. It looked like a glittering castle and was filled with books on every subject. Sapphire could tell that Twilight had painted this, which made it even more of a treasure.

A pair of big black sunglasses rolled out of some green

tissue paper. Sapphire read the note and was surprised to discover that they were from Shamrock. He was always very studious, so she would have expected him to send a book on bugs or stars or rocks. But glamourous sunglasses? She opened his note and read, "Dear Sapphire—Don't forget to protect your eyes! You're going to be out on the lake all day swimming, and high up in the mountains hiking. It's important to wear sunglasses. I've been reading about this inventor . . ." The note went on to describe the inventor of sunglasses, but Sapphire put it aside, thinking she would finish it later. She admired the big, dark glasses—and she was happy to find that they looked more like something a movie star would wear than a scientist.

Sapphire hung up Twilight's painting on the cabin wall and had that weird feeling again. Like she was being watched. She looked around and this time spotted three horns bobbing outside one of the cabin windows. Sapphire had little sisters, so she was used to being spied on. She cleared her throat. "I can see you, you know," she said, laughing. Maybe her fellow campers were playing a prank on her!

But before Sapphire could find out, she heard a whistle blow. "All campers to the mess hall steps," a voice boomed over a loudspeaker.

Not wanting to miss out on anything, Sapphire rushed toward the door, forgetting about the horns she'd seen through the window. Seeing Shamrock's sunglasses on the table, she decided to put them on before heading out, and pushed them over her nose with her hoof.

Other campers smiled at her as she joined the crowd of unicorns in front of the big wooden cabin with a wide front porch. She saw a sign swinging above the doors that read MESS HALL.

Sapphire found a place on the grass where she could see the older unicorns lined up on the porch, as if it were a stage. Sapphire was a little shorter than most unicorns her age, so she stood apart a little, up on the hill so she could see. Most of the counselors were teenagers, and they all looked *cool* with their colorful lanyards and whistles hanging around their necks. One unicorn wore a baseball hat, one wore a bandanna, and one wore black sunglasses, kind of like Sapphire's. Sapphire insistently felt cooler and made a mental note to thank Shamrock for thinking of them, even if glamour wasn't quite what he'd had in mind.

"Welcome to the mess hall! That's what we call the dining hall here at camp. It's where we'll eat all our meals and gather at the start of each day. I know you've all met your cabinmates. . . ."

Sapphire realized that all the other campers were standing in groups. *Everyone must be standing with their cabinmates,* she thought, felling a little worried. She hadn't even met her cabinmates yet! Now she was the only one standing alone. *Did I arrive too late?* Sapphire couldn't help but feel like she was starting off on the wrong hoof. She hoped she hadn't already messed up her chances of being the next Amelia Hoofheart.

Sapphire was surprised when the whistle blew once more, announcing the end of the welcome meeting. The counselors dismissed them and said for everyone to go back to their cabins to get unpacked. She had been so busy worrying about doing things wrong that she hadn't focused on anything the counselor was saying! Sapphire took a deep breath and hoped her cabinmates would be there when she got back. She was determined to make a good first impression.

READ & LEARN

with
simon kids

Keep your child reading, learning,
and having fun with Simon Kids!

A one-stop shop where you can
**find downloadable resources, watch interactive author
videos, browse books by reading level, and more!**

**Visit us at
SimonandSchusterPublishing.com/ReadandLearn/**

And follow us @SimonKids

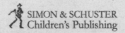

SIMON & SCHUSTER
Children's Publishing